Inspired by a true story.

To my friend Ainhoa, who is different,
SHE'S THE MOST MARVELOUS GIRL IN THE WORLD!

José Carlos Andrés

To those who dedicate their lives to ensuring
that childhood is a happy time, whatever the circumstances...

Lucía Serrano

Ruby the Rambunctious
Somos8 Series

© Text: José Carlos Andrés, 2022
© Illustrations: Lucía Serrano, 2022
© Edition: NubeOcho, 2023
www.nubeocho.com · hello@nubeocho.com

Original title: *Ainhoa Revoltosa*
Translation: Cecilia Ross, 2022
English Editing: Caroline Dookie, Rebecca Packard

First edition: April, 2023
ISBN: 978-84-18599-98-9
Legal deposit: M-11008-2022

Printed in Portugal.

RUBY
the Rambunctious

José Carlos Andrés

Lucía Serrano

nubeOCHO

Ruby was a little girl who fell down a lot.

When she danced, she fell down. When she ran, she fell down.

When she went to the bakery, she fell down.

Everyone thought she was clumsy – her parents, her brothers, the baker... even her!

Ruby's parents were worried about her, so they took her to a variety of different doctors.

Finally, one doctor explained that their daughter's muscles didn't work well.

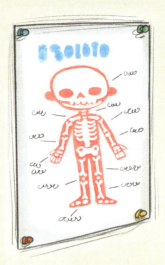

That's why she was always falling down.

Ruby was so happy she started dancing and singing,

"I'm not clumsy! I'm not clumsy! I'm not clumsy!"

After that, her parents began acting very strangely.

If Ruby jumped on the sofa, they said nothing.

But if her older brother snapped off the tip of his pencil on purpose, or if her younger brother picked his nose, they got told off.

"Why don't you ever tell me off anymore?
Don't you care about me?"

Then she had an idea... She took down her dad's
favorite painting and drew all over it!

"RUBY?!" her father shouted,
and his face turned yellow, green, blue, and red.

But a moment later, he just whispered, "That's OK, honey."

At bath time, Ruby brought her mother's tablet into the tub.

Her mother's face turned red, blue, green, and yellow.

"It's fine, sweetheart," she muttered softly.

Then Ruby took a deep breath and shouted...

Her parents' faces turned as red as tomatoes,
as red as red bell peppers, as red as the apple from
Snow White (which was very red).

And for the first time in a long while,
they started laughing.

Then her little brother said,
"But Ruby, you *are* different."

Ruby's face went as white as milk.

There was total silence.

But her little brother pressed on.

"You are different. You're the most rambunctious of us all!"

At that, Ruby started laughing, and she chased him all around the room.

Then Ruby had to stop laughing, because her parents scolded her for having wrecked the tablet and destroyed the painting.

But she didn't mind, because they were finally treating her the same as her brothers, even though she was different – she really was the most rambunctious of the three.

More time passed, and Ruby's parents got her a wheelchair.

She still falls down sometimes, but it's not because she's clumsy – it's because she's always moving a mile a minute!

A ramp was installed at the entrance to her apartment building so that Ruby could go in and out by herself.

Sometimes they used the ramp as an outer space launch pad...

...and other times it was the starting line for a wild and crazy race to school.

Things changed little by little.

But Ruby is still the same...